Grimm's Fairy Tales

The Sleeping Beauty

Written by Saviour Pirotta
Illustrated by Cecilia Johansson

ORCHARD

Grimm's Fairy Tales

For Aunt Teresa
S.P.

For Jessica
C.J.

ORCHARD BOOKS
338 Euston Road, London NW1 3BH
Orchard Books Australia
Level 17/207 Kent Street, Sydney, NSW 2000

This text was first published in the form of a gift collection called
The Sleeping Princess by Orchard Books in 2002

This edition first published in hardback in 2012
First paperback publication in 2013

ISBN 978 1 40830 829 5 (hardback)
ISBN 978 1 40830 830 1 (paperback)

Text © Saviour Pirotta 2002
Illustrations © Cecilia Johansson 2012

The rights of Saviour Pirotta to be identified as the author and
Cecilia Johansson to be identified as the illustrator of this work
have been asserted by them in accordance
with the Copyright, Designs and Patents Act, 1988.

A CIP catalogue record for this book is available
from the British Library.

1 3 5 7 9 10 8 6 4 2 (hardback)
1 3 5 7 9 10 8 6 4 2 (paperback)

Printed in China

Orchard Books is a division of Hachette Children's Books,
an Hachette UK company.
www.hachette.co.uk

Once there were a king and queen of
a faraway country who had everything
they could possibly want. There was only
one thing missing in their lives: a son or
daughter to inherit their kingdom.

"How I wish I had a child," sighed the queen as she walked alone in the royal gardens.

Just then, a frog jumped out in her path.

"Do not be sad," croaked the frog. "Before long you will have a child."

And he was right. A year later the queen gave birth to a baby girl.

The king was overjoyed and ordered a great christening feast.

He invited all the nobles of the land.
The fairies were invited too so they would
present his daughter with magic gifts.

"But we can't invite all thirteen of them,"
said the queen. "We have only twelve
golden dishes."

Preparations for the feast began and
soon the day of the christening arrived.
The twelve invited fairies gathered beside the
baby's cradle.

"I give you the gift of wisdom," said
the first fairy.

"I give you beauty," said the second fairy.

"And I give you strength," said the third fairy.

One by one, the other fairies stepped forward. "I give you confidence."

10

"I give you patience."

"Friendliness."

"Health."

"Love."

"Happiness."

"Riches."

"Kindness."

11

Soon only the twelfth fairy remained to present her gift.

She was about to speak when there came a clap of thunder and the thirteenth, uninvited, fairy flew into the room.

"Good evening, Your Majesties," she rasped. "I've come to give the little princess a very special gift. When she is fifteen years old, she will prick her finger on a spindle – and die."

Everyone in the room gasped. The wicked fairy looked around in triumph, then disappeared with another clap of thunder.

The twelfth fairy stepped forward. "Your Majesty," she said to the queen, "I still have to give the princess my gift. I can't reverse the curse, for my magic is not strong enough. But I can soften it.

"The princess will not die when she pricks her finger on the spindle; she will merely fall asleep for one hundred years."

The very next day, the king ordered all the spinning wheels in the country to be burned.

Time passed and everyone forgot about
the curse.

On the morning of her fifteenth birthday,
the princess went to explore parts of the
palace she had never been to before.

Soon she came to a curious tower with a narrow staircase. At the top was a door, and behind the door was a dusty little room.

"Hello, my dear!"

The princess jumped. There was an old lady sitting in the corner of the room, dressed entirely in black.

"What are you doing?" asked the princess.
"Spinning," said the old lady, twirling the
wheel on a strange machine.

The princess came closer to have a better look.

The old woman smiled. "That's the spindle," she said. "You can touch it if you like."

"Ouch," the princess cried, as she pricked herself on the sharp spindle and a drop of blood mushroomed on her finger.

"Happy birthday, my dear," cackled the old woman who was, of course, the wicked fairy in disguise.

The princess fell onto a couch, at once lost in deep sleep. Almost instantly, everyone else in the palace fell asleep too.

Before long a thick hedge of thorny
bushes grew around the palace, shutting
it off from the world.

Years passed, and the hedge grew as
thick as a forest.

Many people tried to slash their way through, hoping to find the palace and the princess who was said to be sleeping within. But no one succeeded.

Then, almost one hundred years later,
a prince from a faraway country came
by on his brown charger.

The prince had heard about the Sleeping
Beauty and he got off his horse.
He managed to somehow get through
the hedge and to the palace.

He began to explore, stepping carefully over the people and animals asleep in the palace.

At last he found himself in a little tower room. There was a spinning wheel in the corner and on the couch lay the Sleeping Beauty.

She looked so beautiful, the prince couldn't help himself. He bent down and kissed her on the lips.

The princess stirred and opened her eyes.

"You're here, at last," she whispered.
The prince looked so handsome that the
princess fell in love with him straight away.

The prince helped the princess to her feet and they walked slowly down the narrow stairs, hand in hand.

As they moved from room to room, everyone in the palace gradually woke up.

The prince and the princess were married right there and then, and lived happily and contentedly for the rest of their lives.